I
Roy

W9-AMN-745

Here's what kids, parents, and teachers have to say to Ron Roy, author of the A to Z Mysteries series:

"I think your books are the best, and I am a big fan of you."—Michael D.

"Sometimes I don't even know my mom is talking to me when I am reading one of your stories."—Julianna W.

"Your books are famous to me."—Logan W.

"I think if you're not that busy, you could do every letter again."—Abigail D.

"I credit your books as one of the main influences that turned [my daughter] from a listener to a voracious reader."—Andrew C.

"Your letters to the readers at the end of books encourage the children to become part of the writing process."—Jan C.

This book is dedicated to Marie O. and Zeke R.
—R.R.

To the unsung A to Z art directors:
Sue, Joanne, and Rebecca
—J.S.G.

Text copyright © 2005 by Ron Roy
Illustrations copyright © 2005 by John Steven Gurney
All rights reserved under International and Pan-American Copyright
Conventions. Published in the United States by Random House
Children's Books, a division of Random House, Inc., New York, and
simultaneously in Canada by Random House of Canada Limited, Toronto.

www.randomhouse.com/kids
www.ronroy.com

Library of Congress Cataloging-in-Publication Data
Roy, Ron.
The zombie zone / by Ron Roy ; illustrated by John Steven Gurney.
   p.   cm. — (A to Z mysteries) "A Stepping Stone Book."
SUMMARY: Reports of zombies and grave robbers alarm the people of a
Louisiana swampland village, but Ruth Rose, Josh, and Dink begin to suspect
that the supernatural might not be the cause of the eerie occurrences.
ISBN 0-375-82483-9 (trade) — ISBN 0-375-92483-3 (lib. bdg.)
[1. Zombies—Fiction. 2. Cemeteries—Fiction. 3. Swamps—Fiction.
4. New Orleans (La.)—Fiction. 5. Mystery and detective stories—Fiction.]
I. Gurney, John, ill. II. Title. III. Series: Roy, Ron. A to Z mysteries.
PZ7.R8139Zo 2005 [Fic]—dc22 2004004025

Printed in the United States of America First Edition 10 9 8 7 6 5 4 3

A to Z Mysteries®

The Zombie Zone

by **Ron Roy**

illustrated by
John Steven Gurney

A STEPPING STONE BOOK™

Random House 🏠 New York

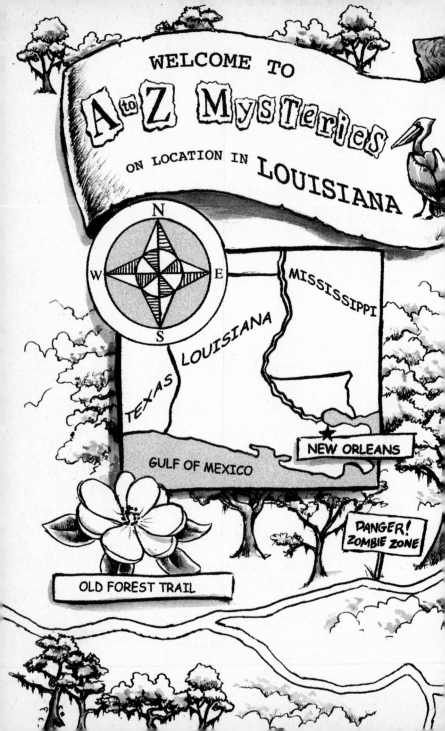

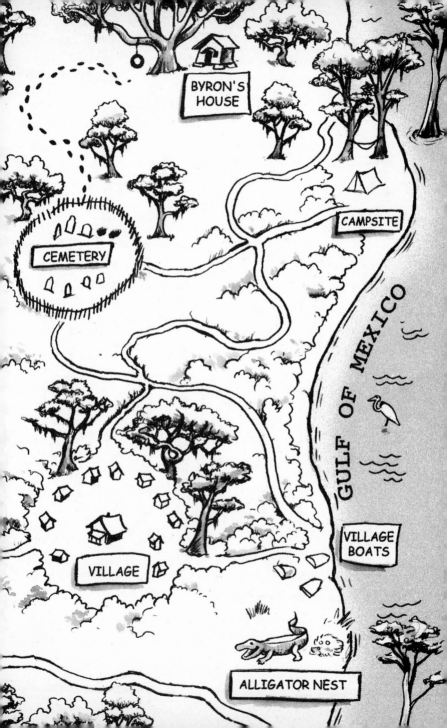

CHAPTER 1

Ruth Rose's grandmother set her paint box on the sidewalk in front of their hotel.

They were in New Orleans, Louisiana. Ruth Rose's gram was visiting the city to take a painting course, and she had invited Dink, Josh, and Ruth Rose to join her.

"What are you going to paint today?" Ruth Rose asked her grandmother.

Ruth Rose liked to dress in one color, and today's color was robin's egg blue. Everything matched perfectly, down to her blue socks and sneakers.

"I don't know yet," her grandmother said. "Our art teacher will tell us. I'd love to paint one of these charming old buildings with the balconies and creeping ivy."

"Thanks again for bringing us," Dink said. His real name was Donald David Duncan, but ever since he was little, his nickname had been Dink.

"And thanks for hiring Jack to show us the bayous," Josh added.

"You're very welcome," Ruth Rose's grandmother said. "Where is he taking you today?"

"We're going on a hike," Josh said.

"We're visiting a community in the woods," Ruth Rose said. "He said the people there live in huts with no electricity!"

"That sounds fascinating!" Ruth Rose's grandmother said. "Oh, here's

Jack's van. Have fun and I'll see you for lunch!"

The kids watched Ruth Rose's grandmother stride away with her paint box under one arm.

A van pulled up to the curb. It was painted all over with trees and vines and flowers. On one side was an alligator with the words GATOR GUIDES spilling out of its mouth.

A tall man in boots, shorts, and a T-shirt hopped out. He had light hair and a deep tan. "Hey, kids, ready for a nice hike?" he said.

"Hi, Jack!" the kids said. Josh and Ruth Rose piled into the back of the van as Jack climbed into the driver's seat. Dink sat in the front passenger seat.

"Buckle up!" Jack said.

While the kids fastened their seat belts, Jack handed Dink a can of bug spray. "There will be a lot of flying critters where we're going," he said.

The kids sprayed their arms and legs while Jack guided the van through the busy city. Dink saw a lot of people jogging, walking dogs, or eating breakfast at little sidewalk tables. One woman strolled along with a parrot on her shoulder!

"We'll be hiking through a beautiful forest today," Jack told the kids as he drove. "And we'll meet those people I told you about."

"Why don't they live in the city like everyone else?" Ruth Rose asked.

"Not everyone likes city life," Jack explained. "The folks you'll meet today would rather live the old-fashioned way. They grow most of their own food and hunt or fish for the rest."

"But don't they miss TV and computers?" Josh asked.

Jack laughed. "The kids go to school in town, so they probably know about that stuff," he said.

"But without electricity, how do they cook?" Dink asked.

"On open fires," Jack said. "Most of them have simple stoves made from clay and rocks."

Dink pictured his parents cooking all their meals outside. He smiled.

The road became narrower until the van was bumping along over gravel. Tall trees lined the road. Grayish green Spanish moss dripped from the branches. Through the open windows Dink could hear birds and smell sweet dampness.

Jack's cell phone started ringing. He pulled the van to the side of the road and stopped to chat for a minute.

"That was my wife," he told the kids after he hung up. "We're expecting our first baby any day now!"

"Cool!" Josh said as Jack continued driving. "Will you take him on hikes?"

"The baby could just as easily be a

girl, you know, Josh," Ruth Rose said.

"Either way, he or she will definitely be a hiker," Jack said, grinning.

Soon Jack parked the van in a small clearing off the road. Behind them was the sunny gravel road. In front was a dark wall of trees, moss, and thick shrubbery.

The kids and Jack climbed out of the van. The air felt muggy, and tiny bugs flew around their faces.

Jack slung his pack over one shoulder. Then he pointed to a brass plaque. The words OLD FOREST TRAIL had been stamped into the metal.

"Here's where the trail starts," he said. "Watch the ground for tree roots!"

"Are there any snakes around here?" Josh asked, stepping quickly to stay right behind Jack.

"Probably," Jack said. "But we won't see them. As soon as they feel our footsteps, they'll take off."

They walked single file. Jack was first, with Josh on his heels. Ruth Rose followed Josh, with Dink in the rear. The trail was narrow and it curved around trees. Moss hung in their faces and roots tried to trip them. The buzz of insects was everywhere.

Dink's skin felt sweaty. He noticed a few narrower trails leading off to the right and left. He was peering down one of these when suddenly he tripped, landing on his hands and knees.

"You all right?" Jack said when he turned around.

When Dink looked up, he saw a small sign nailed to a tree trunk. Some-one had painted three words in red:

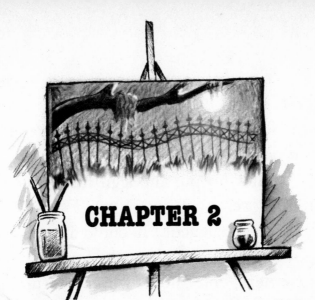

CHAPTER 2

They stared at the sign. Some of the paint had dripped down, giving the words a creepy look. Dink felt the hair on his arms stand up.

"Zombie zone?" Josh said, almost in a whisper. "What does *that* mean?"

"Beats me," Jack said. "I've never seen this sign before, and I bring hikers out here a lot."

Jack moved closer to the sign. "This nail looks new," he said. "See, it hasn't had a chance to rust yet."

"It looks like they used blood," Dink said.

Jack touched a letter. "No, it's just red paint."

"But who put the sign here?" asked Ruth Rose.

Jack shrugged. "It could be a joke, just something to scare the tourists who hike here," he said. "I've heard rumors that strange things have been happening around the cemetery near the village."

Josh gulped. "What kind of strange things?" he asked.

"Well, some people swear they saw a zombie," he said. "Zombies are part of the voodoo religion. I don't know anyone who practices voodoo, but some people still believe in it. Let's keep walking."

As the kids followed Jack, Dink thought about what he had told them about zombies. He felt goose bumps crawl up and down his arms.

They hiked in silence for another few minutes. The dim trail widened into a sunny clearing. About twenty huts formed a half circle around the edges. Each hut had a porch, a garden, and a fire pit or homemade stove.

The hut walls were made of logs, branches, and mud. The roofs had been built with sheets of tin, branches, and broad leaves.

In the center of the clearing sat a larger building. It was at least four times as big as the others. Dink peeked inside the open door and saw a lot of seats. He figured it was some kind of meeting place for the villagers.

"Huh, that's strange," Jack said. "No one's here."

Dink looked around, seeing no one in the gardens or on the porches. The only sounds were the insects and birds

in the trees behind the huts.

"Maybe the zombie stole everyone," Josh whispered. He poked Dink in the back.

"Don't get creepy," Ruth Rose said.

Dink tapped Jack on the arm. "There's someone," he said, pointing.

A tall woman had stepped out of one of the huts and stood on the porch. Her gray hair fell almost to her waist. She wore a long dress that looked home-made. Her feet were bare.

"Hello, Myrna," Jack called. "I'd like you to meet Dink, Josh, and Ruth Rose. They're here on vacation. Where is everyone?"

The woman named Myrna nodded at the kids. She pointed toward a small trail to the left of her hut. "They're all in there, looking at the graves," she said.

Jack looked where she pointed.

"In the cemetery? Why?" Jack asked.

Myrna shook her head. "You go see," she said. "Very bad voodoo." Then she turned and walked back into her hut.

"What's going on?" Dink asked.

"I don't know, but let's go find out," Jack said.

Jack led the kids past Myrna's garden. They left the sunlit clearing and entered the woods on the shady path.

A few minutes later, they came to a small cemetery. It was enclosed by an old iron fence. Moss from a tree branch covered part of the fence. Inside the cemetery, about thirty people were clustered in a bunch. Some of the people were shouting. A few were crying.

"What're they doing?" Ruth Rose asked.

"I'll find out," Jack said. He walked over to the group, with the kids following. Jack knelt on a pile of red dirt next to an old man. In front of them both were two deep holes in the ground.

"Two graves have been robbed this week," the old man said to Jack. "My wife and I are afraid. She wants us to leave here now. She says we can't stay near zombies."

CHAPTER 3

Jack stood up, brushing red clay from his knees.

"This isn't a good time for us to be here," he said quietly to the kids. "Let's walk down to the water."

He led them down a narrow trail. It ended in a sandy clearing at the edge of a bay.

"I heard that man say zombies robbed those graves," Josh said. "But I thought zombies weren't real!"

"I don't believe in them," Jack said. "There must be another explanation."

"But who could have dug up the graves?" asked Ruth Rose.

"I don't know," Jack said.

"Maybe the grave robber is the same person who put up that sign we saw," Dink said.

Jack nodded. "Maybe," he said. He waved an arm toward the water. "Nice view, huh?"

The water was blue and still. Across the bay, they could see tall buildings on what looked like islands.

"Who owns those boats?" Josh asked Jack. A few yards away, several wooden boats had been left on the beach.

"The villagers," Jack said. "They fish and catch crabs out here."

"Is this the Atlantic Ocean?" Dink asked.

"No, it's part of the Gulf of Mexico," Jack said. He pointed out toward some of the islands. "The Gulf joins the

Atlantic way past there, at the tip of Florida."

Jack took the kids on a hike along the water's edge. They saw long-legged blue herons wading in the shallow water. Small fish darted away from the herons' shadows. Jack pointed to a deer lying in the shade.

"It's so beautiful here," Ruth Rose said. "And so quiet!"

"I agree," Jack said. "I'd love to buy a piece of this land and build a house here."

He opened his pack and pulled out four small bottles of water. They all sat on a log and sipped, watching the herons search for fish.

Across the water, the sun flashed gold against the distant buildings.

"How'd you like to camp out here tonight?" Jack asked. "We can cook our supper over a campfire."

"Excellent!" Josh said.

"I'll ask my grandmother at lunch," Ruth Rose said. "But I know she'll say yes!"

"Great! After I drop you off, I'll do some grocery shopping," Jack said.

After their water break, Jack showed the kids how to identify different birds' nests. He taught them how to spot poison ivy. He explained how to make tea and medicines from some plants.

Jack looked at his watch. "You guys must be getting hungry," he said. "It's time to go back to town."

"I'm starving!" Josh said. "I don't know if I can last till we get back to the hotel!"

Dink laughed. "Well, you could always grab a raw fish like that heron," he said.

A half hour later, the kids met up with Ruth Rose's grandmother in the hotel's outside restaurant. She was sitting under an umbrella on the balcony that overlooked the street.

"Gram, can we go camping with Jack tonight?" Ruth Rose asked her.

"Of course," her grandmother said just as the waiter appeared at their table.

Everyone ordered cheeseburgers and lemonade. While they waited for their food, the kids told Ruth Rose's grandmother about the zombie sign and the grave robber.

"Who would steal dead bodies?" Ruth Rose asked.

"People have been robbing graves for different reasons all through history," her grandmother explained. "Sometimes robbers were searching for valuables that were buried with the bodies. Hundreds of years ago, a famous painter stole bodies so he could study the muscles and bones. He wanted his paintings

of people to look as real as possible."

"Gross!" Josh said.

At a nearby table, two men in suits and ties were drinking iced tea. Dink noticed that one of them kept glancing at their table. To Dink, it seemed as if he was trying to overhear what Ruth Rose's grandmother was saying.

Just then the waiter showed up with their food. No one talked about dead bodies as they ate.

The next time Dink looked up, the two men were gone.

CHAPTER 4

At four o'clock the kids were waiting in front of the hotel. Jack's van showed up a few minutes later.

Jack opened the rear doors. "I brought a tent big enough for all three of you," he told them.

"Where will you sleep?" Ruth Rose asked.

"In this." Jack showed them a rolled-up string hammock.

They all climbed in and buckled up. Jack joined the late-afternoon traffic.

"Where are we going to camp?" Dink

asked. He was sitting in the back with Josh, and Ruth Rose was up front with Jack.

"How about near the water?" Jack asked. "Tomorrow morning, I'll take you to see an alligator nest."

"They make nests?" Josh said. "Like birds?"

"Not like birds. Mother alligators lay their eggs on the ground and cover them with vegetation," Jack explained.

Jack parked his van at the head of the trail. Between the four of them, they managed to carry the tent, Jack's hammock, and two small food coolers.

They took a different trail to the bay this time, and soon came to the clearing at the water's edge.

"Just dump everything near the boats," Jack said. "We'll get your tent set up before it gets dark."

Josh peeked under one of the

upside-down boats. "There are no alligators here, right, Jack?" he asked.

"No, it's too open," he said. "But
they often hunt at night. When it gets
darker, look for two yellow spots in the
water. Alligator eyes reflect light, so our
campfire will help us see them."

As Jack and the kids set up camp,
their shadows grew longer. Soon the sun
was behind the trees.

After the tent was up, Jack hung his
hammock between two trees. He gave
the kids some containers. "Fill these
with water," he said.

"We have to drink salt water?" Josh
asked. "Yucko!"

"No, we'll need it to put out our
campfire later tonight," Jack explained.
"I brought bottled water for drinking."

The kids walked to the water, which
was only about twenty feet from their
tent.

As Josh stooped to fill his jug, Dink

dropped his hand on Josh's shoulder. "Is that an alligator?" he whispered. "I see two eyes!"

"Duh," Josh said. "I guess I can tell a floating branch from a reptile!"

Ruth Rose joined in. "But . . . but that branch is swimming toward you!"

"Very funny," Josh said. He lugged his container back to Jack.

"Just set the water by that tree," Jack said as he scooped a depression in the sand. He made a wall around it with rocks and damp sand.

Then the kids helped him find dead twigs and branches. Soon they were sitting around a cheery blaze. The dancing flames made all their faces look ghostly. Dink thought of zombies and alligators. He scooted a little closer to the fire.

"Okay, who wants hot dogs, lemonade, and marshmallows?" Jack asked.

"We do!" Josh yelled.

Jack opened the coolers and began

pulling out tons of food.

The kids roasted their dogs and ate them by the fire. By the time they had finished their marshmallows, stars were visible. The moon was full and partly hidden by clouds. A few lights flickered way out in the Gulf.

Dink was the first one to yawn. Then everyone else started yawning. They covered the fire embers with sand, and Jack doused the pit with water from the bay.

"Sleep tight," he said as the kids crawled into the tent.

"You guys can sleep near the opening," Josh said. He crawled to the farthest end of the roomy tent.

"Why?" Dink asked. "You usually like to sleep by the door."

Josh pulled off his shirt and used it for a pillow. "Yeah, but this way if an alligator crawls in here," he said, "he'll eat you and Ruth Rose first!"

Later, Dink suddenly sat up in the tent. A noise had wakened him. He listened, then peered out through the zippered opening.

Moonlight through the trees cast shadows on their campsite.

Then Dink saw a tiny light moving in the woods. Dink's first thought was that he was seeing fireflies. But he knew that fireflies didn't travel in a straight line. He woke Josh and Ruth Rose.

They both rubbed their eyes, then joined Dink on their knees at the tent opening.

The light was still there, bouncing along in the trees.

"What do you suppose it is?" whispered Ruth Rose.

"A flashlight," Dink answered.

"Who would be sneaking around in the middle of the night?" Josh asked.

Dink put out his hand and silently unzipped the tent flap. "Let's go find out," he said.

"Maybe we should wake up Jack," Josh said. "It could be the zombie!"

"I have a feeling that zombies don't carry flashlights," Dink said.

The kids stuck to a narrow path as they moved slowly toward the light. The moon played hide-and-seek with the clouds. One moment it beamed down on them, the next it was gone.

As they watched, the distant light would disappear, then glow again, only to vanish once more.

The kids came to a spot where three trails crossed each other. They could turn right or left or go straight forward.

"Which way?" asked Josh.

"The middle one seems to head where the light was," Dink said.

"Guys, that path goes to the cemetery!" Ruth Rose said.

"OMIGOSH!" Josh croaked. "Maybe we're following the grave robber!"

"And if we hurry, we can catch him!" Ruth Rose said.

"I'm not catching *anybody!*" Josh said.

"Let's keep moving," Dink said. "If we find anything out, we'll go back and wake up Jack. He'll call the cops on his cell phone."

The kids crept forward. Ruth Rose had been right. At the end of the trail, Dink saw gravestones glinting in the moonlight.

The kids stopped in the shadow of a

giant oak tree, thirty yards from the graveyard. The moonlight touched the fence and the gravestones. The two empty graves were black holes with mounds of dirt piled next to them. Nothing moved.

"I guess I was wrong," Dink whispered. "I thought for sure—"

Suddenly Josh slapped his hand over Dink's mouth. Then Dink heard Ruth Rose gasp.

One of the empty graves was glowing! As the kids watched, two hands emerged, grabbing at the edge of the hole.

Then a head appeared. Whoever it was held a small flashlight in his mouth. The beam jumped crazily as a dark figure pulled himself up and out of the grave.

Silently, Dink, Josh, and Ruth Rose dropped to the ground.

CHAPTER 5

The man standing at the grave's edge was tall. He wore dark clothing. His face was in shadow, but his hair looked silver in the moonlight. Dink felt there was something familiar about him.

The man wiped red clay from his pant legs. Then he shone the flashlight on his wrist, causing his watch to gleam briefly. He turned and disappeared into the trees.

"Wh-who was that?" Josh asked.

"It sure wasn't a zombie wearing a watch and carrying a flashlight," Ruth Rose said.

"I wonder what he was doing down

in that grave," Dink said. "Should we go look?"

"No!" Josh hissed. "It's bad enough we're creeping around cemeteries. We're not crawling down into some grave!"

"Let's go tell Jack," Ruth Rose said.

The kids retraced their steps back to the campsite. Dink was relieved to see Jack's tall form lying in the hammock.

"Let's not wake him," Dink said. "We can tell him in the morning."

The kids tiptoed past Jack, then knelt to crawl into the tent.

"See anything interesting?" Jack asked.

All three kids jumped and whipped around. "You're awake?" Dink said.

Jack sat up in his hammock. "I'm a light sleeper," he said. "Where have you been?"

"We need to talk to you," Ruth Rose said. "We saw someone at the cemetery!"

"You did?" Jack jumped out of his hammock. He had put on dark sweat clothes. He pushed up his sleeve and looked at his watch. "What were you doing at the cemetery at midnight?"

"Something woke me up," Dink said. "I noticed a light in the woods, and we decided to follow it."

Dink stared at Jack. He couldn't help comparing him with the man they'd just seen at the graveyard. Both were tall, wearing dark clothing. Both had light hair and wore wristwatches.

"We saw a guy crawl out of a grave!" Josh said. "We know he wasn't a zombie 'cause he was wearing a watch. Right, guys?"

Dink focused on Jack's face. Could it have been him they'd just spied on? What would Jack be doing in an empty grave?

"Do you think it could have been the

grave robber?" asked Ruth Rose.

"Was he digging?" Jack asked.

"We don't know," Josh said. "We didn't see a shovel or anything."

Josh pointed at Dink. "He wanted to go down in it, but I said no way!"

"You were smart," Jack told Josh. "But you were all pretty foolish to go out in these woods without telling me. Don't do it again, okay?"

The kids nodded. "Okay, but who do you think that was?" Ruth Rose asked.

Jack stretched and leaned against one of his hammock trees. "My guess? One of the men from the village just checking out the cemetery. For all we know, they may have posted guards to make sure the grave robber doesn't steal anymore," he said.

"But what was he doing down in one of the graves?" Josh asked.

Jack shrugged. "I have no idea," he

admitted. "Now how about we get some sleep?"

Jack hoisted himself back into his hammock. The kids crawled into the tent, and Dink zipped it shut. After they were settled, Dink lay on his back staring at the tent ceiling.

He tried to remember if he'd taken a good look at Jack's hammock before they'd followed the flashlight. Dink didn't know for sure if Jack had been there when they'd left.

Dink tried to swallow, but his mouth had gone dry. Could the grave robber have been sleeping in a hammock just outside their tent?

Dink didn't sleep well that night.

CHAPTER 6

Dink woke up when he heard someone singing outside the tent. He peeked out and saw Jack opening the coolers.

Sunlight slanted across the water, turning the Gulf to gold. A sweet-smelling breeze came with the sun. It was a perfect morning, and Dink was hungry.

As Dink pulled on his sneakers, he thought of last night. He laughed. No way could that have been Jack in the grave. No way.

Dink nudged Josh and Ruth Rose

awake, then unzipped the flap and left the tent.

Jack was wearing shorts and a T-shirt again. "Hey," he said, smiling at Dink. "I brought fruit and bagels and juice. You hungry?"

"Yeah, my stomach is rumbling," Dink said.

"Mine is, too!" Josh said, joining them. Ruth Rose came next, fixing her headband.

Jack carried the food down to one of the flat-bottomed boats to use it as a tabletop. They looked out over the water as they ate.

"Look," Jack said, pointing along the shore. A mother squirrel and two young ones were sitting at the water's edge. They washed their hands and faces, then waddled back into the trees.

"When are we going to go see the alligator nest?" Josh asked.

Jack checked his watch. "Pretty soon. But I want to check in on Myrna first. Do you mind?" he asked. "She seemed worried yesterday."

"Sure," Dink said. "But what will we do with the tent and stuff?"

"I'll get it later," Jack said.

"Are you going to tell Myrna what we saw last night?" asked Ruth Rose.

Jack chewed his lower lip for a few seconds. "If I'm right and it was one of the village men, she'd already know about it," he said. "But I'll definitely mention it to her."

The kids helped Jack tidy up. Then they hiked toward the small village. Myrna was there, weeding her garden.

Myrna looked up at Jack. "Everyone is at the graveyard," she said.

"I came to see how you're doing," Jack told her.

Myrna sat on the edge of her porch.

She stretched her back and wiped dirt from her hands. "My friend Bo wants to leave here. One of the robbed graves is his father's." She glanced up at Jack. "I am worried, too."

Just then Jack's cell phone rang.

He answered, listened, then said, "Okay, hon, see you in a few minutes."

"Is the baby coming?" asked Dink.

"I don't know, but my wife said she feels funny," Jack said. "She wants to go see her doctor. Do you mind if I take you back to the hotel for a while? I'll pick you up later and we can check out that alligator nest."

"They can stay with me," Myrna offered. "Go see your wife. The kids will be fine here until you get back."

"Is that okay with you guys?" Jack asked.

"Sure," Ruth Rose said. "But will you let my grandmother know? She keeps her cell phone with her while she's painting."

Jack nodded. "I'll call her from the van," he said.

He took off jogging back toward the trail. "See you in an hour!" he called over his shoulder.

"I'd better finish this weeding,"

Myrna said. She hiked her dress up and got down on her knees in the garden. The bottoms of her feet were black from the rich soil.

"Myrna, did one of the men go out to guard the cemetery last night?" Dink asked.

The woman sat back. "Why are you asking?"

"Uh . . . Jack was going to ask you, but he forgot," Dink said.

Myrna shook her head. "I don't know. Listen, while I work on the garden, why don't you kids go out and explore?" she said.

"What if we get lost?" Josh asked.

"Then I'll come get you," Myrna said, reaching into a deep pocket and pulling out a whistle on a lanyard.

"My grandkids use this when they come to visit me," she said, dropping the lanyard around Josh's neck.

"Don't your grandchildren live here?" Dink asked.

Myrna shook her head. "My son took his family and moved away," she said, gazing at her simple hut.

Myrna yanked a weed from in between some clumps of lettuce. "Go play for a while," she said.

The kids left Myrna and walked to the edge of the clearing.

"I want to go back to the cemetery," Ruth Rose said.

"Yuck! Why?" Josh asked.

"Aren't you curious?" Ruth Rose asked. "Or do you believe we saw a zombie last night?"

"I don't know and I don't care," Josh said. "That totally creeped me out."

"Oh, come on, Josh," Dink said. "Now that it's daylight, we might find a clue to who was down in that grave."

"Okay, I'll go, but don't try to get me to climb down in it!" Josh said.

The kids found the path to the grave-yard. When they got there, they saw dozens of village people on their knees near the two empty graves. Their heads were bowed, and no one was saying a word.

"I think they're praying," Dink whispered. "Let's keep going."

They moved quietly away, following the iron fence.

They came to the beginning of another narrow path, opposite the one that led back to Myrna's hut.

Josh peered down the path. He was holding on to Myrna's whistle with one hand. "What's down there?" he asked nervously.

"That's what we're going to find out," Ruth Rose said.

They walked single file. Ruth Rose led, and Josh hiked right behind her—which was why he nearly walked up her heels when she suddenly stopped.

"What?" Dink asked when he was standing next to Ruth Rose.

Ruth Rose didn't say anything. She was pointing to the ground.

Then Dink and Josh saw it, too. Ruth Rose had spotted a large footprint in the moist red clay.

"Ooooh my gosh," Josh moaned. "Zombie feet!"

CHAPTER 7

"Look, there's another one!" Dink said, pointing ahead on the path. "And another!"

"I wonder who made them," Ruth Rose said. She knelt down and put her finger in one of the prints. "These are toe marks. Did you guys notice if that guy in the grave was barefooted?"

Dink shrugged. He put his own foot next to the print. "It's nearly twice as long as mine!"

"Let's follow them," Ruth Rose said.

Josh nearly choked. "Are you crazy?"

"Josh, don't you want to know whose feet these are?" Dink asked. "It could be the grave robber!"

"Come on," Ruth Rose said, taking the lead again.

As they walked the trail, the soil changed from dark red to brown to almost black. They had no trouble finding more footprints in the soft earth.

Suddenly Josh stopped. He stuck his nose into the air like a wolf. "I smell food," he said.

"What?" Dink asked. "Hot dogs?"

Josh shook his head. "Something sort of spicy," he said. "Like chili!"

"Chili in the woods?" Dink asked. "Gee, maybe there's a restaurant out here in the middle of nowhere."

The next one to stop suddenly was Ruth Rose. She put a finger to her lips. "Shhh, listen!" she hissed.

A few seconds later, they all heard a

thunk. Then there were more *thunk*s.

The kids stared at each other with raised eyebrows. Ruth Rose kept walking and the others followed.

The trail ended in a sunny clearing. Dink, Josh, and Ruth Rose stood and gaped. Straight ahead was a small cabin built from stuff you'd find in a junkyard: old hunks of tin, mismatched boards, sheets of plastic, even the rusted hood of a car. The cabin was raised off the ground on thick tree stumps.

A gigantic tree shaded the house. Dink noticed a tire swing hanging from one of the branches. He wondered if kids lived here.

Standing with his back to them was a tall man holding an ax. His hair was so light it looked white. He wore long pants and a long-sleeved shirt. Below the pant bottoms, Dink could make out large bare feet.

The man raised the ax over his head and brought it down on a log. When he bent to grab the two split pieces, he noticed the kids watching him.

Dink was surprised. He had expected an older man. But the face staring at them was smooth. The man had warm brown eyes. He looked no older than Jack.

"Hello," the man said. His voice was deep but gentle. "Are you lost?"

Dink spoke up. "No, we're . . . exploring," he said.

"Are you hungry?" the tall man asked.

Behind the stack of firewood, a fire was burning in a pit. A black iron pot was suspended over the flames, and the smell of something spicy filled the air.

"We just had breakfast," Ruth Rose said. "But thank you anyway, mister."

"My name is Byron," the man said.

"I'm Ruth Rose, and these are my friends Dink and Josh," Ruth Rose said.

Dink saw an easel set up under a tree. "Can we look at your painting?" he asked.

"Okay," Byron said, blushing.

The three kids walked over to the easel. Byron had painted an old iron fence. Hanging over the fence was a tree branch dripping gray Spanish moss. The moon shone down, bathing the scene with a soft glow. The space behind the fence was blank.

"It's not finished yet," Byron said from behind Dink, startling him.

How could such a big guy walk so silently? Dink wondered.

CHAPTER 8

"Your picture is excellent!" Ruth Rose said. "My grandmother likes to paint, too."

Byron smiled and blushed. He walked toward his little garden. "Do you like strawberries?"

"Sure!" Josh said, and the kids followed Byron.

The garden was neatly laid out in rows. A shovel and hoe stood leaning against a small tree. There were tomatoes, lettuce, cucumbers, and some things Dink didn't recognize. One corner of the garden was filled with strawberry plants.

Byron told Dink, Josh, and Ruth Rose to help themselves. The kids waded into the patch carefully as they picked the bright red berries.

Suddenly they heard a *whoosh,* and a large owl flew out of the trees. The bird landed on Byron's wrist and plucked a strawberry from his hand.

"This is Bill," the man said.

"He's awesome!" Josh said.

Byron stretched his arm toward Josh. "You can pet him," he said proudly.

While Josh was petting Bill, Ruth Rose poked Dink on the arm. When he looked at her, she nodded toward the shovel a few feet away.

The edges of the shovel blade were caked with red clay.

Byron carried Bill over to the soup pot. The kids watched him scoop out something and feed it to the owl.

"That red dirt looks the same as the dirt at the graveyard!" Ruth Rose whispered.

"So what?" Josh said, plucking another berry from the patch.

"Josh, that could mean Byron was digging in the cemetery," she said, keeping her voice low. "The soil here in his garden is black, not red!"

Josh's hand stopped halfway to his mouth. His eyes shut, then flew open again. "You mean . . . that could have been *him* in the cemetery last night!"

"Not so loud!" Dink whispered. "Guys, I'm sure there's red clay in other places around here, not just in the cemetery. I saw the same color clay on the floor of Jack's van yesterday."

Josh stole a look at Byron, who was still feeding Bill. "That guy we saw last night had light hair like Byron's," he whispered. "And look at his big feet. He could have made those footprints we saw near the cemetery."

"None of that proves anything," Dink said.

He remembered Jack in the moonlight last night. Jack's blond hair had looked silvery, the same as the hair of the mystery man in the cemetery. "I have some other ideas," Dink added quietly.

Just then Byron looked up and smiled at the kids. "Do you want to swing on my tire?" he asked.

"N-no, thank you," Ruth Rose said. "We have to be getting back."

Byron tossed Bill into the air and the bird disappeared in the trees. Then Byron walked toward the kids and stretched out a huge hand. "It was very nice meeting you," he said.

Dink shook Byron's hand. Beneath the skin Dink felt the man's strength.

"It was nice meeting you, too," Dink said.

The kids walked toward the trail. When Byron and the cabin were out of sight, they began running. Five minutes later, they stopped, panting, in front of Myrna's little hut.

Myrna was sitting on her porch talking with a woman dressed in shorts and a T-shirt.

"Did you kids have fun?" Myrna asked.

"Yes!" Josh said. "We met a big guy

named Byron and his owl."

"He showed us his painting," Ruth Rose said. "He sure is a good artist."

Myrna nodded. "Byron makes his own paints from nature," she said. "He gathers berries, digs up roots, anything he can find. He grinds the stuff up to create his different colors."

Myrna introduced the woman to the kids. "Lucy is a friend of Jack's," she said. "She'll drive you back to your hotel."

Lucy smiled at the kids. "Jack's at the hospital with his wife," she said. "Looks like today is the day for the baby to be born."

They said good-bye to Myrna and followed Lucy to the trail. They had only gone a short distance when they saw a man approaching them. He was hurrying toward the village.

When the man noticed Lucy and the

kids, he stopped. His face was red and sweaty. "Am I on the right trail for the village?" he asked.

The man was wearing a straw hat, dressy pants, and a striped shirt. His briefcase and shiny black shoes looked out of place in the forest.

Even with the hat, Dink recognized

the man. He had been sitting near them at the hotel restaurant yesterday. What was he doing in the woods?

"Yes, about another five minutes straight ahead," Lucy said. Then she added, "Is anyone expecting you?"

"Yes," the man said, then hurried on his way.

"That's odd," Lucy said after the man left them. She chuckled. "If he's a salesman, he'll have a hard time selling anything!"

They kept walking. When they passed the zombie sign, Dink asked Lucy about it.

"I have no idea what that means or who put it there," Lucy said.

"Jack thought it might be a joke," Ruth Rose said.

"Not very funny," Lucy said. "A lot of people who live near these parts believe in zombies."

CHAPTER 9

Lucy dropped the kids off, and they traipsed into the hotel.

"What are we gonna do about Byron?" Josh asked. "I think he dug up those graves, and I think he was the guy we saw in the cemetery last night!"

"Let's talk upstairs," Dink said quietly.

They took the elevator. On their floor, Ruth Rose unlocked the room she shared with her grandmother.

"Here's what I think," Dink said, sitting on the carpet. "The man we saw in the cemetery last night might have dug up those two graves, but we don't know that for sure."

Josh and Ruth Rose plopped down next to Dink.

"And we don't know if the guy we saw was Byron, either," Dink went on.

"Well, I think it was Byron," Josh said. "Who else could it be?"

"How about Jack?" Dink asked. "He's tall, and he has light hair like the man in the cemetery."

"Jack?" Ruth Rose said. "But he was sleeping in his hammock."

"Did you actually *see* him in the hammock when we left?" Dink asked. "Jack could've gone to the cemetery after we were asleep and made it back to the campsite before we did."

Josh shook his head. "Why would Jack be down inside that grave?" he asked.

"I don't know," Dink said. "But I

don't know why Byron would, either."

"I just thought of someone else with light hair," Ruth Rose said.

Dink and Josh looked at her.

"That man we passed on the trail with Lucy," she said. "He was wearing that funny hat, but underneath, his hair was kind of grayish white."

"And you know what else?" Dink said. "He and another guy were sitting in the restaurant when we had lunch with your grandmother yesterday!"

"So?" said Josh.

"Well, they seemed pretty interested when we were talking about zombies and stuff," Dink said.

Josh laughed. "Who wouldn't be?" he said.

Just then the kids heard a light *thump* coming from the hallway. They froze, all staring at the doorknob as it slowly turned.

Suddenly the door swung open and Ruth Rose's grandmother walked in.

"What's the matter with you three?" she asked, setting down her paint box. "You look like you've seen a ghost!"

"Gram, you scared us!" Ruth Rose cried.

"Me? I'm just a harmless old lady! So how was the sleep-out with Jack?" she asked.

"We had a nice time, Gram," Ruth Rose said. "We've just been trying to figure out who robbed those graves."

Ruth Rose's grandmother sat on her bed and kicked off her sandals. "Can I help?" she asked.

Ruth Rose told her grandmother all about going to the cemetery last night, and about the man they saw crawling out of the grave.

"My word!" her grandmother said. "Did you tell Jack what you saw?"

"Yes," Dink said. "He said it was probably one of the men from the village guarding the cemetery."

"Dink thinks the guy we saw was Jack," Josh said.

"I didn't say it was Jack," Dink responded. "I said it could be. The person in the grave was tall and he had light hair and dark clothes. Just like Jack."

"And just like Byron," Josh said.

Ruth Rose's grandmother looked at Josh. "Now, who is Byron?" she asked.

"He's this man we met after Jack

took his wife to the hospital this morning," Ruth Rose said.

"Yes, Jack kindly called me and let me know you'd be staying in the village with someone called Myrna Sanchez," her grandmother said. "But you decided to go back to the cemetery, right?"

"We wanted to look for clues," Ruth Rose said. "But the villagers were all in the cemetery, so we followed some footprints. They led right to a cabin in the woods. That's where we met Byron and his owl, Bill."

"I think Byron's the guy we saw in the graveyard," Josh interrupted. "I think he stole those coffins, too, because there was red dirt on his shovel just like the clay in the cemetery!"

Finally, Ruth Rose told her grandmother about the man they had met on the path. "It could have been him, too," she said. "He had light hair, and he seemed pretty interested in the village."

Dink mentioned that the same man had been eating lunch near them yesterday. "I think he was trying to hear what we were saying," he said.

"Okay, you've mentioned three different men who are tall with light hair," Ruth Rose's gram said. "One of them could be the man you saw last night. What I don't understand is why any of them would have any interest in that cemetery."

"I just thought of something," Dink said. "When we walked down to the water with Jack, he told us he'd love to buy a piece of that land."

Everyone was staring at Dink.

"What if Jack put up that sign and dug up the graves to scare the villagers?" Dink continued. "If they left, maybe he'd be able to buy their land."

CHAPTER 10

"Well, I still think Byron did it," Josh said. He stuck up three fingers. "One, there's red clay on his shovel. Two, he could have left those huge footprints we saw. Three, he's a painter, so he could have painted that sign."

"Byron paints?" asked Ruth Rose's grandmother.

"We only saw one painting," Ruth Rose said, "but it was real good."

Ruth Rose's grandmother reached for her sandals. "I have a hard time imagining that Jack is involved with grave robbing," she said. "But I would very much like to meet Byron!"

They flagged down a taxi in front of the hotel. Dink told the driver they wanted to go to the Old Forest Trail.

"Got it!" the driver said as she moved smoothly into the late-afternoon traffic.

Ten minutes later, Ruth Rose's grandmother paid the driver. "Will you pick us up right here in an hour?" she asked.

"Sure thing," the driver said. She waved and drove away.

Ruth Rose's grandmother looked at the dark and dense forest in front of them. "Are you sure there's a trail in here?" she asked.

Josh showed her the plaque. "Don't worry about snakes!" he said bravely.

"I wasn't even thinking about snakes until you mentioned them!" Ruth Rose's grandmother said.

This time Josh led the way as they

hiked the trail. They stopped when they came to the zombie sign.

"That *is* strange," Ruth Rose's grandmother said. "Someone definitely wants people to think there are zombies around here."

"We think it's the same guy who dug up the graves!" Ruth Rose said.

Her grandmother nodded. "What a busy little zombie!"

They hiked on and soon came to Myrna's village. No one was around.

"Look, they're all in that big hut," Dink said, pointing to the largest of the buildings.

The door was open and the kids could see people sitting on benches. Dink heard a voice speaking firmly.

"They're having some kind of meeting," Ruth Rose said. "Maybe it has something to do with the dug-up graves."

"Is it very far to Byron's cabin from

here?" her grandmother asked.

"No," Dink said, pointing. "That trail goes to the cemetery, and then you take a little path to where Byron lives."

The three kids led Ruth Rose's grandmother down the trail. They stopped at the little cemetery.

"Someone worked hard to dig those graves up," Ruth Rose's grandmother commented, pointing to the mounds of red dirt near the two empty holes.

"See, Gram, that's the same clay we saw on Byron's shovel," Ruth Rose said.

"Yes, but I would assume red clay could be found in other places," her grandmother said.

They continued walking. A few minutes later, they stood in the trees behind Byron's cabin.

"I don't see him," Ruth Rose whispered, peering around a tree trunk.

"Why don't we just go knock on his

door?" her grandmother suggested.

Josh giggled. "I don't know if he even *has* a door!" he said.

"Come on," Dink said. He stepped into the sunshine. The foursome walked around the cabin.

Byron was standing in front of his easel with a brush in his hand. Small jars of paint were lined up on the easel's tray.

"Hi, Byron," Dink said.

Byron turned around quickly. He had a blob of white paint on his chin. When he saw the kids, he broke into a wide smile.

"This is Mrs. Hathaway, my grandmother," Ruth Rose told Byron.

Byron picked up a cloth to wipe his hands. Putting out one hand, he said, "Hello, I am very pleased to meet you."

"I've heard a lot about you," Ruth Rose's grandmother said with a warm

smile. "May I look at your painting?"

Byron blushed. "I have better ones in my house," he said.

They all studied Byron's painting. Since this morning, Byron had added something. He had painted tombstones inside the fence. Now Dink recognized the iron fence.

It was the fence at the cemetery.

"I think you are a truly wonderful painter," Ruth Rose's grandmother told Byron.

"This is the cemetery, isn't it?" Dink asked Byron.

The tall man nodded. "I like it there," he said.

"Do you go there a lot?" Dink asked.

"Bill likes to hunt mice at night," Byron said. "Sometimes I go with him. I sit by the cemetery. It's peaceful there."

"Did you ever see anyone digging in the cemetery?" Dink asked.

Suddenly Byron's face grew red. He put his brush down. "I didn't mean to steal it," he said.

"Steal what?" asked Ruth Rose.

Byron walked into his cabin and came back holding something in his hand. It was a man's leather wallet.

"I was sitting by the cemetery last week. It was dark, and Bill was hunting," Byron said. "Two men came and dug up the graves. They carried the coffins away. When they were gone, I found this in the dirt. I saved it for them, but they didn't come back."

"That's what the guy was doing in the grave last night!" Josh said. "Looking for his wallet!"

Ruth Rose's grandmother took the wallet and looked inside. "How nice," she said. "He even has his picture on his business card."

The kids looked at the white card.

The name Jay Frisk was printed in big black letters. Below the name it said LAND DEVELOPER, with a phone number and an e-mail address.

Next to the name was a small picture of the man they'd passed on the path.

"I get it," Dink said. "This guy dug up those graves to scare the villagers into selling their land!"

"Now everything makes sense!" Josh said. "This Frisk guy is the zombie! He probably put up that sign, too!"

"What should we do?" Dink said.

Ruth Rose's grandmother whipped out her cell phone. She dialed information, then said, "The New Orleans Police Department, please."

JAY FRISK
LAND DEVELOPER
504-555-9662
jfrisk@friskmail.com

CHAPTER 11

The next morning, Jack picked up the kids after breakfast. Ruth Rose was wearing pink from headband to sneakers.

"You look like a sunrise," Jack told her.

"Thanks, Jack," Ruth Rose said. "Was your baby born yet?"

"Yes!" the proud father said. "It's a beautiful little girl. Theresa and her mom are sleeping, so now's our chance to get a peek at the alligator nest."

A half hour later, they were all hunkered down in some bushes near the water. Jack had brought binoculars, and they were taking turns peering at a mother alligator.

She was lying half in the water with her long snout pointed toward her nest. The gator's scaly hide was blackish green, ridged and bumpy like a truck tire.

"I don't see any babies," whispered Josh.

"They haven't hatched yet," Jack said, pointing to a small hill of vegetation. "That mound is her nest. The eggs are buried in that stuff."

"Why isn't she sitting on the nest?" Ruth Rose asked. "Won't the eggs get cold?"

"The rotting vegetation keeps the eggs warm," Jack explained. "Mama gator is watching the water in case a meal swims by."

The large mother alligator lay as still

as a log. Her mouth was partly open, and every now and then her eyes would blink.

"You kids did a good job figuring out who robbed those graves," Jack said. "The villagers reburied the coffins and had a nice ceremony. The cops took the two developers in for some serious questions. They won't be trying to scam any more people."

"Do you think the people in the village were really going to sell their land?" Dink asked.

"They would have eventually," Jack said. "My guess is that if the robbed graves didn't convince them, the scammers would have tried something else next time. They were greedy guys who wanted to build high-rise apartments there."

"If Byron hadn't been out with his owl, he never would have seen those men," Josh said. "Or found that wallet."

Jack smiled. "Byron told Myrna that he's been on his own since his parents abandoned him when he was eight years old. Never went to school, just lived in these woods. Myrna and the villagers are building him a new hut near hers. He's going to live with them now."

"And Byron gave my grandmother one of his paintings," Ruth Rose said. "She showed it to a man who owns an art gallery. He said Byron is going to make a ton of money!"

Jack put his finger to his lips. "Listen," he whispered.

They all heard high, croaky noises coming from the nest.

"Now watch," Jack said.

The mother alligator began moving toward the mound. When she got there, she scraped away the top layer of the vegetation.

Twenty or thirty tiny green-and-yellow alligators were crawling out of their eggs. As they freed themselves, they wriggled toward their mother.

"Now check this out," Jack said quietly.

The mama alligator flattened herself on the ground with her jaws opened. The babies scrambled over her bottom jaw, right into her mouth!

"Is she going to eat them?" Josh asked.

Jack laughed. "No, that's how mama alligators and crocodiles protect their babies," he said. "They're safe inside her mouth."

"Protect them from what?" asked Ruth Rose, taking her turn with the binoculars.

"There are a lot of critters who would love to snack on a baby alligator," Jack said. "Raccoons, possums, herons, you name it. When Mama thinks it's

safe, she'll open her mouth and her babies will crawl out."

The four backed quietly away and headed for the trail.

"Speaking of lunch," Josh said as they hiked, "I'm hungry!"

"Josh, no one was talking about lunch," Dink said.

Josh grinned. "Now we are!" he said.

THE END

A to Z Mysteries

Dear Readers,

About seven years ago I had an idea for a mystery about an author who disappears. I decided to call the book *The Absent Author*. Since then, I have written 25 more mysteries for kids. And now, with *The Zombie Zone*, the series is complete. What a wonderful time I have had dreaming up plots and mysteries and crimes to keep my readers entertained!

No series can be written without a lot of people getting involved. I would like to thank all the people at Random House who supported my writing and my ideas. But most of all, I am grateful to you, my readers, for choosing my books to read. Thank you also for your letters, e-mails, and suggestions over the years.

So many of you have sent suggestions for the last few titles. Thank you! One of the words that kept popping up for the Z book was *zombie!* Whenever I read or hear that word, I

Ms. Gabbart's class of A to Z fans!

get all shivery. I have learned that kids love to read scary books, as long as they're not too scary . . . so I came up with *The Zombie Zone.* It was fun for me to write, and I hope it gave you pleasure to read . . . and a few goose bumps!

Thank you, and happy reading!
Sincerely,

Ron Roy

P.S. Please keep visiting my Web site at www.ronroy.com!

**Have you read every book
in the A to Z Mysteries series?
See how it all began!
Collect clues with Dink, Josh, and Ruth Rose
in their *first* exciting adventure,**

THE ABSENT AUTHOR

Finally Dink got up and walked out.

Josh and Ruth Rose were waiting for him.

"What's the matter?" Ruth Rose said. "You look sick!"

"I *am* sick," Dink mumbled. "I invited him here. It's all my fault."

"What's all your fault?" Josh asked.

"This!" he said, thrusting the letter into Josh's hands. "Wallis Wallace has been *kidnapped*!"

Track down all these books
for a little mystery in your life!

A to Z Mysteries®
by Ron Roy

Capital Mysteries
by Ron Roy
Who Cloned the President?
Kidnapped at the Capital
The Skeleton in the Smithsonian
A Spy in the White House

The Case of the Elevator Duck
by Polly Berrien Berends

Ghost Horse
by George Edward Stanley

Check out Ron Roy's brand-new series about KC and Marshall in Washington, D.C.!

Capital Mysteries

When the President of the United States starts acting funny on TV, KC decides he's not the *real* President Thornton. She's sure he's a clone!

KC's mom and President Thornton have disappeared during the Cherry Blossom Festival. They were kidnapped—right under the bodyguards' noses!

Leonard Fisher claims he's the heir to the Smithsonian fortune. If KC and Marshall can't prove he's a liar, Washington will lose its world-famous museums!

KC's mom is marrying the President of the United States, or is she? The wedding may be canceled because someone keeps leaking the secrets!